SKATERS VERSUS DEBATERS!

Nichelle said a silent prayer before she opened her hand and checked the size of her straw. *Whew! A long one. No candidacy for Nichelle.* She gazed around the table to see who'd gotten the short straw. The answer was immediately clear. Andy was looking down at his straw, horrified.

"Duude!" his friend Evan said with a grin.

At the table behind them, Megan was being similarly congratulated. "You go, girl!" shouted one of the debaters. "Megan — our next vice president!"

Thomas looked over to see what was happening at Nichelle's table. When he saw that Andy had drawn the short straw, he broke into a huge grin. The others at his table began to laugh harder than ever.

"All riiight!" Megan Graham squealed. "You guys have found the candidate for the ages! A worthy opponent!"

"No backing out now," admonished Thomas with a chuckle. "This is perfect. It'll be the skaters versus the debaters."

Andy just sat there staring at his short straw.

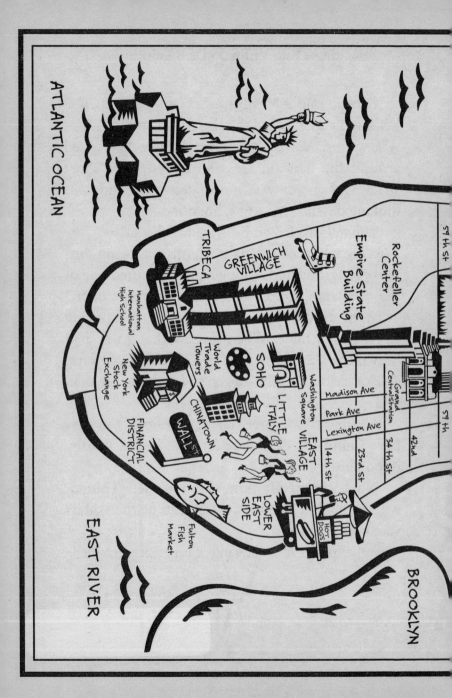

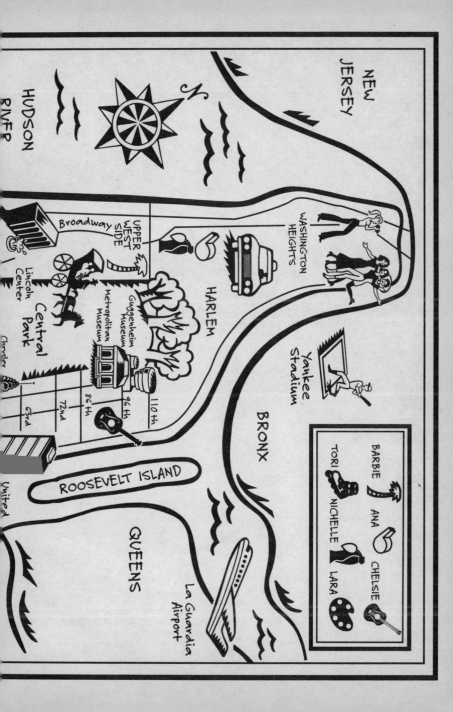

GENERATI*N
GIRL

#12

Campaign

Chaos

By Melanie Stewart

A GOLD KEY PAPERBACK
Golden Books Publishing Company, Inc.
New York

A GOLD KEY Paperback Original

Golden Books Publishing Company, Inc.
888 Seventh Avenue
New York, NY 10106

BARBIE, GENERATION GIRL, and associated trademarks are owned by and used under license from Mattel, Inc. © 2000 Mattel, Inc. All Rights Reserved.

Polaroid trade dress is used with permission of Polaroid Corporation.

Cover photography by Graham Kuhn

Interior art by Amy Bryant

No part of this book may be reproduced or copied in any form without written permission from Golden Books Publishing Company, Inc.

GOLD KEY is a registered trademark of Golden Books Publishing Company, Inc.

ISBN: 0-307-23461-4

First Gold Key paperback printing March 2000

10 9 8 7 6 5 4 3 2 1

Printed in the U.S.A.

GENERATI✳N GIRL

| Campaign |

| Chaos |

Chapter 1

A Real Date?

Nichelle Williams and her good friends Tori Burns and Ana Suarez threaded their way through the crowd at International High School in New York City. The last bell had just rung and students were streaming into the halls. Kids were everywhere, going in all directions. Their laughter, conversation, and shouts added up to a cheerful background roar. I. H. was one of the largest and newest schools in New York, and it was an exciting place to be.

Nichelle raised her voice to be heard over the din. She was giving her friends a rundown of all the homework she had to get through that night.

"There's Spanish — fifteen conjugations, one for every year of my *life*, for heaven's sake! A book report in music appreciation. And enough math problems to last me until I'm thirty. And it's only Monday!"

"Don't talk to me about homework, mate," Tori interrupted. "Remember, I'm in your maths class, too. Your problems are my problems."

Nichelle couldn't keep from grinning. Tori always referred to the subject as "maths," the way everyone did in her native Australia. Their friend Chelsie, who came from England, did the same.

"That's easy for you to say," Nichelle gently chided her friend. "You're a math whiz."

"Oh, and *you're* not?" Tori shot back, giving her an I-can't-believe-you-said-that roll of her sky-blue eyes. "What's the difference in our maths averages? Maybe a tenth of a point?"

"Okay, okay," Nichelle conceded sheepishly. "It's not that any one subject is so hard. It's just that I've got so much work piling up this week. There's a biology lab, a music test, and — the latest and worst — a six-page paper for American history. You know what a stickler Mr. Budge is. And he seems to expect even more from me since Barbie and I did that special project on the African Slave Burial Ground here in Manhattan."

"Crikey, Nichelle," exclaimed Tori, "you don't think he expects you to top that, do you? That was awesome."

"I don't know," Nichelle muttered. "It's just that I hate handing in anything less than my best work."

"Whoa," said Tori, grabbing Nichelle's wrist and forcing her to stop. "That's a different story. That's not *Budge* pressuring you, that's *you* pressuring you."

"Maybe you're right," Nichelle said with sigh.

"Look," said Tori softly. "If it would help, we could knock off the maths problems together on the phone tonight."

"And I could help you with your Spanish homework," chimed in Ana, a Mexican-American who spoke Spanish fluently.

Nichelle gave her friends one of her signature bright smiles. "You guys are the best," she said. "Thanks, but I'll be all right." She ran her long fingers through her springy dark curls. "I'll just turn myself into a homework machine."

"Funny," replied Ana. "You don't look like any homework machine I've ever seen."

3

Ana was right. Nichelle looked, in fact, just like what she was: an up-and-coming teen model. Her long limbs, sculpted cheekbones, flawless cinnamon skin, and clear dark eyes ringed with long curly lashes had won her several important modeling contracts recently.

Nichelle loved modeling. In fact, she loved her whole life — even the schoolwork. She just had to get that history paper under control.

"Let's talk about something else," Nichelle suggested.

"I can't talk any more at all," Ana said. "I have to be in my suit and in the pool for swim team practice in exactly thirteen minutes. See you tomorrow. Call me tonight, Nichelle. Adios!" And off she sprinted.

"Crikey, that girl is dedicated. She'll go to the Olympics one day, for sure," Tori said admiringly.

"Hey, there's Barbie, heading our way," said Nichelle.

Barbie Roberts, an exchange student from Malibu High, was easy to spot in any crowd. Her ever-ready smile seemed to shout California sunshine even on a gloomy March afternoon. An aspiring actress, Barbie also worked behind the

4

camera. More than once, her talent with the video camera had helped her friends out of various jams.

Barbie rushed toward her friends. "Guess what I heard in gym class just now," she began breathlessly.

"What?"

"Matthew Choy is moving to Brazil with his family!"

"Crikey, he's one of the best kids in this school," said Tori sorrowfully. "Smart, funny, *and* he knew all the words to 'Louie Louie.'"

"That really is too bad," Nichelle agreed. She and Tori and Matt Choy served together on the student council. Matt was vice president, and she and Tori were the sophomore class representatives. Nichelle knew that Matt was one of the few kids on the student council who could actually get things done. Turning to Tori, she said, "Remember when he convinced Principal Simmons to create a student position on the PTA? And when he helped us organize the time capsule project?"

Tori nodded vigorously. "So many of the other kids on the council only seemed to care about making their records look good for college. Matt really wanted to make a difference."

"Who's going to take Matt's place?" Barbie wondered aloud.

"I don't know," replied Nichelle. "But I sure hope it isn't left open. We really need a strong replacement. Not one of those 'I'm too cool' slacker types."

Barbie looked at her watch. "Uh-oh, I've got to go," she said. "Chelsie asked me to write a farewell piece about Matt for the school paper and the deadline is tonight at 6 P.M. You know how serious Chelsie is. She can't extend *Generation Beat* deadlines, even for friends."

Nichelle laughed. "Just a wee bit disorganized," she said. "But serious all the same."

The others laughed, too. Their beloved Chelsie was always just a bit frayed around the edges, but she did care so very much about the quality of the school newspaper, on which she served as senior editor. "I'd better get to work," said Barbie. "Call me tonight."

"I've got to get going, too," Tori said, heading for the stairwell. "And don't forget to ring me up if you want to split up the maths."

"Okay, bye," Nichelle called after her.

"Bye?" questioned a deep pleasant voice behind her. "Why, you haven't even said hello."

Nichelle turned and found herself looking up into the smiling face of Thomas Garie. He was one of the few boys in the school who made Nichelle feel short. Short *and* flustered.

Thomas was just so poised and cool and handsome. Especially handsome. An African-American like Nichelle, he had the trim good looks of a track star, which he was. He dressed like an Ivy League student, which he surely would be next year. And as a senior, he was one of the most popular and respected boys in the school.

He was also a great dancer. Nichelle knew this firsthand because they'd gone to the Autumn Dance together in November. But they hadn't seen each other much since then. Nichelle certainly hadn't been pining away in the meantime; her life was too full for that. Still, she did sometimes wonder what he thought about her. Did he like her as much as it had seemed last fall? Had he found a girlfriend? Perhaps he no longer thought a mere sophomore worthy of his attention. She quickly put those questions out of her mind, because he clearly seemed to be paying attention now.

"I believe I owe you an apology," Thomas began. "I've been meaning to call you for a while, but I've been crazy with schoolwork. They really pile it on us seniors. And of course, the whole winter was just crazy with the college application thing."

"You poor baby," murmured Nichelle. "Everybody knows Yale is just dying for you."

"Oh, I don't know," he said modestly. "I'll know in a couple of weeks. Fat envelope for yes, thin one for no. Meanwhile, I'm just trying to keep up with my homework."

"Sophomores get their share, too, you know," Nichelle said. "In fact, I have to do a monster paper on the Westward Expansion for Budge's class. He's expecting something extra special, too, and I'm stumped."

"We're talking about the mid-nineteenth century?"

Nichelle nodded.

"I know just the thing!" Thomas said, leaning close enough that Nichelle could smell his cologne. "There's a collection of rare and old maps at the main branch of the New York Public Library. Just include some information from an original pioneer map, and ol' Budge will hand you an A on a silver platter. I promise. Hey, I'm on my way to the library myself. Want to come along?"

"Uh —" Nichelle hesitated, remembering her heavy homework load. She did some lightning-fast mental calculations. If she did her math problems on the phone with Tori and worked on her conjugations with Ana, she could probably afford to spend an hour or so at the library. She was going to have to do it sometime this week anyway, she rationalized. "Okay, sure," Nichelle said at last.

"Great!" Thomas exclaimed.

Nichelle gulped. *Is this a date or what?* Beneath her calm exterior, her heart was beating fast.

Outside, under a heavy gray sky, groups of kids were gathered in front of the school. Most of them happened to be upperclassmen whom she didn't know. But it seemed that every one of them knew and liked Thomas.

"Hey, Tom!"

"Thomas! My man!"

"Thomas! Call me later, okay?"

There were so many greetings called out to him that Nichelle felt almost invisible, which was not a feeling she was accustomed to. Usually, *she* was the popular one. This threw her a bit off balance.

Then, from somewhere to her right, she heard

the rumble of a skateboard and a familiar sort of mumble. "*Hey, N'chelle.*"

It was Andy, one of the "Pants Boys." At least that's what Nichelle and her friends called Andy Groebner and Evan Hadden, the two cute skateboarders who wore their pants so low that you couldn't help wondering if they'd stay up. The mumbly way the Pants Boys spoke was another source of amusement. At the beginning of the school year, it was only their European friend Lara Morelli-Strauss who'd been able to understand their strange mutterings. By now, thanks to practice, everyone in Nichelle's group could make out a lot of what the Pants Boys were saying. And the surprise was, they often said quite interesting things — just in a really strange way.

Anyway, Nichelle was pleased to hear a friendly "hi" hurled in her direction, especially amid the hail of greetings Thomas was getting.

Without breaking stride, turning his head, or even really moving his lips, Thomas said to Nichelle, "You don't hang out with any of those geeks, do you? They could ruin your standing."

"*Geeks?*" said Nichelle, her voice rising in anger.

10

She couldn't quite believe her ears. "What are you saying? Andy is not a gee —"

Thomas winked and flashed her a disarmingly charming smile. "Hey, I was just kidding. Don't take everything so seriously."

Nichelle looked at his face. There seemed to be absolutely no guile in his voice or in his open, good-natured grin. As the light changed, he slid his arm lightly around her shoulder. And they walked that way, silently, to the subway. *Maybe he hadn't meant those remarks the way they had sounded*, she thought. In any event, her momentarily unsettling feelings were quickly blown away in the whoosh of the inbound 1 train.

The rest of the afternoon was a lovely blur. It was always a thrill for Nichelle to walk up the steps of the old main library building, with its two imposing but friendly lions guarding the entrance. She had not yet seen the huge reading room, which had recently been reopened after a long renovation. It was beautiful! The afternoon light filtered in at a slant from the tall windows, falling on the long oak tables with their rows of elegant little reading lamps that gave off individual pools of warm light.

11

Nichelle knew that some of the greatest books in American history had been written right here in this room.

There were perhaps a hundred people in the room, sitting and reading books and newspapers, and they ranged from the wealthiest to the poorest New Yorkers. There were ladies who had mink coats slung over the backs of their chairs, and old men who looked as if they might not have a place to sleep when they left the library. Each one of them was fully absorbed in reading, though. All people were welcome in this palace of the mind.

Nichelle loved the old pioneer maps that Thomas helped her find. They were almost like drawings of the countryside. She imagined pioneer families headed to Oregon or California with nothing more to guide them than some primitive documents. Nichelle thought about them, and then she thought about her own ancestors, who had come to America chained on slave ships. How far her family had come!

After they'd been working about an hour, Thomas leaned toward her. "I'm famished," he whispered. "Could I interest you in some tea? I know a great place that's right around the corner."

"Teatime? That would be simply smashing," she whispered back in a funny imitation of Chelsie's English accent.

They put on their coats and went out into the increasingly nippy air. In a few moments, they had entered a sweet, cozy little restaurant decorated in shades of blue, yellow, and green. The tables were covered with lacy white cloths, and the thin, fine cups and plates sparkled in candlelight. The owner, who was from England, knew Thomas's family because Thomas's mother had spent a year in college studying at Oxford. She brought them their tea and food herself. Nichelle loved the tiny sandwiches and the delicious, flaky scones served with gooey strawberry jam and mounds of clotted cream.

As they ate, Thomas told Nichelle all about his junior year spent as an exchange student in France, his work on the debate team, his plans to visit Africa this summer, his family's sailboat, his older brother who played piano with one of the hottest jazz trios in New York, his summer internship at the United Nations. It went on and on.

Is there anything this guy can't do? Nichelle wondered. Even his jokes were good. And Nichelle was a good judge of jokes.

When it was time to go, Thomas helped Nichelle with her coat, held the door for her, and walked her to her bus.

"I had a wonderful time. The tea was great. Thanks," Nichelle said as her bus pulled in to the stop.

"Let's do it again soon," Thomas answered.

On the ride home, Nichelle's thoughts often drifted from the scene around her. The words "Let's do it again soon" floated through her mind.

As she rang the bell for her stop, Nichelle told herself sharply, "What I have to do soon is get my homework and history paper taken care of."

She quickly walked the two blocks from the bus stop to her house. Even in still-cold March, with the trees black and leafless, her Harlem neighborhood was beautiful. The blocks were lined with historic brownstones, each one different. Nichelle always got a lift when she approached her own front door, which was made of heavy mahogany and had a big brass knocker in the shape of a lion's head. Today the knocker reminded her of the library lions, which brought her mind back to her afternoon with Thomas, and . . .

No, no, no. Work to be done.

With a little help from her friends (after-dinner phone consultations with Ana and Tori), Nichelle had finished all her homework assignments and roughed out an outline for her history paper, using the information she had gotten from the pioneer maps. It was a pretty good outline, if she did say so herself. And she was beginning to feel confident that the paper would be a snap to write. That encounter with Thomas had been fortunate for more than one reason.

With the bit of time she had left before she climbed into bed, she wrote to her favorite cousin in New Orleans. She'd been meaning to do it for weeks and didn't want to put it off any longer.

Dear Niecy,

Thanks for your letter. I can't believe you have flowers blooming down there already.

Did you know that my dad might be visiting you this spring? There's a pediatricians' conference there next month.

In answer to your question, I'm not quite sure whether I am dating anyone right now. Today I went to the library and then had tea with a cool boy. His name is Thomas. He's a senior and he's really, really popular. I went to the Autumn Dance with him, but I haven't seen him much since. I don't know if he has a girlfriend. I hope not.

Do you think that going to the library with a boy counts as a date? Don't forget we went out for tea, too.

I'm so, so glad that you will be coming to visit this summer. You can meet all my friends. Maybe Thomas, too.

Much love from your New York cousin,

Nichelle

P.S. Write back soon.

Chapter 2

A Candidate for the Ages

The next morning Nichelle stuffed her homework into her silver backpack and threw her steel blue overalls on over her favorite yellow tee. She ran downstairs to the kitchen, where the butter yellow walls were glowing in the morning sunlight.

"If you want to ride downtown with me on the subway, you'll have to hurry," said her mother, who was just finishing a quick cup of coffee. "I have an early meeting at the mayor's office."

"You know I want to," said Nichelle. "Let me grab a bagel, and I'll be ready to roll."

Nichelle and her mother loved their subway

rides together. It was one of the nice things about Nichelle's going to I. H., which was within walking distance of City Hall, where her mother worked as an aide to the mayor. Even though they were jammed in with the morning rush hour crowd, they enjoyed the chance to catch up with each other.

Nichelle and her mom talked about Nichelle's trip to the library with Thomas. "I wouldn't get my hopes up *too* much," her mother warned. "High school seniors are like kids holding one-way tickets to new adventures. They may look like they're here, but in reality they're already gone."

"I know, I know," said Nichelle. "He's just so darned good-looking."

"Looks, of course —"

"— Aren't everything," said Nichelle, finishing her mother's sentence. "I know. But they're pretty nice."

"You know, I sometimes run into Thomas's parents at charity functions," said her mother. "His mom seems to be very kind and generous, but his dad can seem a bit standoffish. Almost a snob. Thomas isn't like that, is he?"

Nichelle suddenly winced as she remembered

18

Thomas's not-so-funny "joke" about Andy. "He didn't seem that way last autumn," she said. "I sure hope he isn't now."

In homeroom that morning, the P.A. system clicked on a bit earlier than usual.

"Good morning. This is Principal Simmons," said the voice on the loudspeaker. The kids sat up and listened more attentively than usual. Normally, Assistant Principal Merlin delivered the morning announcements, in a droning voice that sounded like a car straining to start on a sub-zero morning.

Principal Simmons's voice, on the other hand, commanded attention, not just because she was the principal, but because everybody liked her.

"I have something unusual to talk about this morning," she began, "so I thought I'd do the announcements today. First, the regular stuff. 'Tuna Noodle Surprise' for lunch," (groans from the students), "and the drama club would like some new members, so please think about going to their meeting after school today. Second, they're fixing the escalators on Thursday, so you'd better do some wind sprints to get ready." (More and bigger groans.) The school building was so new, it was still full of "bugs," and some days it seemed as if hardly anything worked.

"Now, here's the special thing," continued Principal Simmons. "Many of you know by now that Matt Choy, our student council vice president, is moving away. We wish him well, and we will miss him. He has made a tremendous contribution to this school. And, of course, after he goes, there will be nobody at I. H. who knows all the words to 'Louie Louie.'" Everybody laughed, but the shrieks and whoops from Matt's homeroom down the hall could be heard all over the school.

"Sadly," Principal Simmons went on when the laughter died down, "Matt's departure leaves a huge vacancy on the student council. So I'm proposing that we hold a special election to choose Matt's replacement. Here's how we're going to do it:

"First," she explained, "students may nominate any sophomore, junior, or senior. Yes, you may nominate yourself. You can drop off your nominations at the *Generation Beat* newspaper office, Room 712, or submit them on-line to the I. H. website. You can either post a new nomination or add your name to the list of votes for an already-nominated candidate.

"Second, this Friday morning the four students with the greatest number of votes will be asked to run.

"Third, candidates will have another week, until next Friday, the 13th, to campaign. On that morning, candidates will debate the issues. Following that, voting will take place during the lunch periods and a winner will be announced after the end of seventh period.

"I don't need to remind you how important and serious the election of student council officers is. Please consider nominating the worthiest candidate you know, even if it's you."

Nichelle thought about it. Whom did she know who had the time to take on the vice president's job? She, herself, didn't — that was for sure. And then there was the frustration of dealing with all the people on the student council who weren't interested in doing anything more challenging than holding bake sales and cluttering the halls with posters about school spirit days. The student council needed a good replacement for Matt — that was also for sure.

After first-period biology, Nichelle raced to math class. She wanted to get there early to see

Tori, she told herself. Of course, if she did happen to see Thomas in the hall, there might be time for a quick hello. Nichelle had to laugh at her own ridiculousness. But she hurried just the same.

She met Tori at the door of their math classroom. "Are we still on for Eatz after school?" Tori asked.

Eatz was the restaurant about a block from school where Nichelle and all her friends hung out. The decor was a bit shabby and the food only so-so, but the portions were generous and the ambience terrific. Nichelle especially loved the turkey wrap, and everyone agreed that the cheese fries were the best anywhere.

"Eatz? Sounds great," replied Nichelle. "I'll get there as soon as I can. But I might be late. Budge always keeps talking after the bell rings."

By the time she pushed through the front doors at Eatz, Nichelle was pretty tired. It had been a long day, and Budge had indeed droned on after the bell, while his students filled up page after page of notebook paper. She was so glad to see Tori, Barbie, and Lara waiting for her in their regular tattered, orange-vinyl booth. When she saw that the Pants

Boys were there, too, she immediately broke into a broad smile. How could anyone as smart as Thomas not pick up on how cool they were? Most sophomores, at least, knew that Andy and Evan, for all their mumbling ways, were surprisingly good students. Andy wrote complicated electronic musical compositions that he distributed for free over the Internet. Evan, the shyer of the two, was a technical wizard — someone who read physics books for fun and could build a computer from a ball of string and a box of doughnuts. Nichelle loved the Pants Boys because there was nothing false about them; they treated everyone honestly and fairly, and they knew how to enjoy life to the fullest. She hoped Thomas was just joking.

Nichelle waved to her friends, and as she began making her way across the restaurant, her heart banged in her chest and a sound like rushing water filled her ears. There, in the booth right behind theirs, was Thomas. *Oh, why does he have to be so cute?*

She was sure Thomas hadn't spotted her. He was crowded in with a bunch of other kids from the debate team, facing away from her. *They must be having a meeting,* she thought.

By the time she slid into the booth, Nichelle felt like she'd walked about three miles. The only place left at the table put her about five inches away from Thomas. She could smell that lemony cologne he wore. He still hadn't turned around. The kids in the debate booth were talking loudly and all at once.

"I heard the Saint Michael's debate team is awful," one of them was saying.

"So did I," she heard Thomas say. "We're going to demolish them on Saturday."

"It'll be a piece of cake," agreed another.

Nichelle suddenly became aware of Tori's hand waving in front of her face. "He-llooo?" Tori was saying. "Oh, Nichelle? Are you with us?"

Nichelle had been so busy listening to the conversation at the next table she'd forgotten to say hello.

"Hard day, Nichelle?" Barbie asked. She and Tori, of course, had no idea that Thomas had been on Nichelle's mind so much lately.

Out of the corner of her eye Nichelle could see Thomas turn his head at the mention of her name. Nichelle felt her cheeks burn.

"Just a busy day," she managed to reply to Barbie.

"Me, too," said Barbie. "I hardly had time to think today! And I got yelled at in math class because Sarah Douglas was talking to me. It wasn't even my fault."

"Ugh! That's the worst," said Tori. "Meanwhile, I forgot my English paper, and Mr. Toussaint was not happy."

"Pressure, pressure, pressure," said Nichelle.

"And, of course," said Thomas, who had now turned around to face Nichelle, "you're going to run for vice president of the student council, too, right?"

"Yeah, right," said Nichelle. "That's just what I need."

"*How s'bout you, Tori?*" Andy asked, beating out a complex rhythm on the table with a pencil.

"Me?" Tori replied. "I don't need it either."

"You're just apathetic," interjected a thin, bespectacled boy at the debaters' table.

"I am not!" Tori retorted. "I just haven't got the time."

"Isn't that just the point?" the boy continued. "Who has the time? Nobody. But somebody has to run. It's our civic duty, for crying out loud. We owe it to our school. What if some dweeb got in?" Everybody at the debaters' table laughed.

"Why don't you run, Rick?" Thomas suggested to the boy who had just spoken. "You'd win, no trouble."

"Nah, can't," said Rick, his face turning crimson. "I've got baseball and mixed chorus this spring on top of debate. I'd be stretched kinda thin."

Tori burst out laughing. "Oh, listen to 'Mr. Big Civic Duty' here. All talk, no action. I guess that's what you debaters do best."

"Oh, yeah?" Rick replied angrily. "Well, anybody here at our table is way more qualified to be student council vice president than anybody at your table."

"Oh, yeah?" parried Tori, rising to the challenge. "Well, I can see only two people here who have had any *serious* student government experience, and that's Nichelle and me. And any one of our friends here would make a way better vice president than any of you illywackers."

"*Illy*-what? What did you call us?" Rick asked.

"Ill-y-wack-er," repeated Tori, pronouncing each

syllable slowly and with delicious pleasure. "It's Australian for braggart, phony — a con man."

Nichelle watched as Rick's eyes just about bugged out of his head. "Okay, let's just cool it, guys," she blurted out. "This is going nowhere fast."

"No way," said Rick. "I'm not going to let some stupid sophomore call us illywhatses."

"Hey, Rick, get a grip!" Thomas said in a commanding voice that immediately shut his teammate up. Then he turned to face Nichelle and her friends. "I think I've got a way to settle this dispute amicably," he said. "We'll draw straws. Your table and our table. Whoever gets the short straw at each table agrees to submit his or her name for nomination — with no excuses. Agreed?"

"*No way, man*," said Evan, putting his hands up in front of him.

"What's the matter, you *chicken*?" taunted Rick.

"Nobody here is chicken," Tori exclaimed. "Sophomores rule!"

"Debaters rule!" cried Rick.

Nichelle had a sinking feeling in the pit of her stomach. This situation was spiraling out of control. She glanced around the table. Lara and Barbie, and even the Pants Boys, seemed as disconcerted by this silly bickering as she was, but nobody appeared willing to abandon Tori while her honor was under attack. Nichelle sighed. She knew she wouldn't change her fearless friend for all the world. But sometimes she just wished that Tori was a little less impetuous. All she could think about was how her life would change if she pulled the short straw and was obliged to enter the election campaign.

Megan Graham, a junior girl from the debate team who was sitting next to Thomas, was already taking the wrappers off a bunch of plastic straws from the dispenser on the table. "I happen," she said, "to have a little pair of scissors right in my bag." She waved a pair of dainty nail scissors above her head. "I shall now cut down two of these straws — one for each table." She passed out the straws, a handful to Thomas and a handful to Nichelle, who accepted them reluctantly.

"Okay, you guys," said Megan. "Now, mix 'em up." Nichelle and Thomas each arranged the straws in their hands so the short ones could not be spotted. Amid much nervous laughter, the straws were drawn.

Nichelle said a silent prayer before she opened her hand and checked the size of her straw. *Whew! A long one. No candidacy for Nichelle.* She gazed around the table to see who'd gotten the short straw. The answer was immediately clear. Andy was looking down at his straw, horrified.

"*Duude!*" his friend Evan said with a grin.

At the table behind them, Megan was being similarly congratulated. "You go, girl!" shouted one of the debaters. "Megan — our next vice president!"

Thomas looked over to see what was happening at Nichelle's table. When he saw that Andy had drawn the short straw, he broke into a huge grin. The others at his table began to laugh harder than ever.

"All riiight!" Megan Graham squealed. "You guys have found the candidate for the ages! A worthy opponent!"

"No backing out now," admonished Thomas with a chuckle. "This is perfect. It'll be the skaters versus the debaters."

Andy just sat there staring at his short straw.

When Nichelle and her friends left Eatz a half hour later, they ran into their friend Chelsie just outside. As usual, she was hanging onto a big messy pile of books and papers. Chelsie was a talented journalist and wrote terrific songs. But, boy, was she disorganized.

"How's it going, mate?" Tori asked.

"I'm fine, thanks," she said in her perfectly well-bred English accent. Chelsie's dad was a British diplomat, and her family lived in New York City because of his work. "Guess what?" she said, beaming. "I've just been given the loveliest present."

She pulled a tiny, exquisite, red leather-bound book from her crushed-velvet bag. Stamped on the cover in very fancy gold letters were the words

William Blake
Poems

"William Blake! He's bonzer!" said Tori. She began reciting: " 'Tyger! Tyger! burning bright / In the forests of the night.' He's the most extreme poet, that's why I like him. I found his poems once when I was poking 'round the library in Melbourne."

Chelsie opened the book and showed them the beautiful endpapers that were colored like marble, and the heavy cream-colored pages. There was one poem, beautifully lettered, on each page.

"What a treasure. It looks really old. Is it?" Nichelle asked.

"Indeed. When my mother was younger, she received it from her grandmother. And now she's given it to me."

"Bonzer, mate. That's something great. You'll be able to pass it on to your own daughter someday." Tori giggled. "Maybe I'll be able to give my daughter these skates," she said, pointing to the pair of in-lines she was strapping onto her feet at that moment.

Soon Tori was streaking away down the sidewalk, calling, "Ta-ta!"

"I have to hurry, too. I have an audition," Barbie said. "Acne-cream commercial."

"As if you ever had one zit in your life," laughed Nichelle.

"I'll share a cab with you, Barbie," said Chelsie. "I must be off, too."

Nichelle said good-bye and then walked the couple of blocks to City Hall to meet her mother.

Happily, her mother was able to get out of work on time, and they just missed the worst of rush hour. They even got seats. They always arrived home in a much better mood when that happened.

At home in their big cheerful kitchen, the family made dinner together. Dr. Williams made his famous fruit salad with fresh mint leaves. Mrs. Williams arranged an attractive platter of grilled chicken and vegetables. Nichelle made quick muffins. Her older brother Shawn set the table with their favorite blue dishes and cleaned up after dinner.

Nichelle settled down at the desk in her room and did homework until her eyes wouldn't stay open anymore. Then, just as she was getting into bed, the phone rang. It was Chelsie. She was so upset there were tears in her voice.

"Nichelle, I don't know what to do. Remember that wonderful book of poems I showed you? Well, I was looking for it to find a quote to use in my English paper, and *it's lost!* I've torn my room apart looking for it. It's not here. I'm sure of it."

Nichelle pictured Chelsie's disorderly room. That book could be lost for a long time in that mess.

"Did you check your backpack?" Nichelle asked her.

"About forty times."

"And you looked in your jacket pocket?"

"Too small."

"Let's think about this," said Nichelle. "You had it when we saw you outside Eatz, right?"

"Right," said Chelsie.

"And then you took a cab with Barbie. Did you go right home?"

"Yes! That's it! I must have left it in the cab," Chelsie wailed. "I'll never see it again. How can I tell my mother?"

Nichelle tried to sound calm, although she knew that the situation was bad. "Is there any way you can remember the number of the cab, or the name of the driver?"

More collected now, Chelsie was able to think. "I do remember the driver's name. We were talking about how cold it gets in New York during the winter, and I noticed the name on his license. It made me smile. It was Muhammad Ali — like the famous American boxer. Only, this Muhammad Ali came from Egypt. Oh, Nichelle, do you think I can find him?"

"It's worth a try," Nichelle assured her friend. "We just have to figure out how. Do you remember the name of the cab company?"

"Definitely not. Do you think there's some office that has all the names of all the cab drivers in New York?"

"Brilliant. I know there is, I've read about it. I just can't remember what it's called. Maybe if you call Information they can tell you."

"Okay, I'll try right now. I'll let you know what happens."

"I'm keeping my fingers and toes crossed!"

"Thanks, Nichelle," Chelsie sniffled. "You are a wonderful friend."

As Nichelle drifted off to sleep, she wondered why she'd ever let the "skaters" and the "debaters," as Thomas had put it, square off and draw straws. Andy could get hurt by this insane contest, and that was something she just didn't want to let happen.

Chapter 3

See Andy Run

It was a busy week at I. H. Midterms were on everyone's minds. Even the teachers seemed preoccupied. Nichelle caught an occasional glimpse of Thomas in the halls. He would wave or say hi before hurrying on. But that was it. Seniors were really busy, she knew.

Nichelle began to think that even if the afternoon she had shared with Thomas had been a "date," there would not be another. Her feelings about Thomas were all mixed up. He was so special and exciting. Yet he didn't seem to go out of his way to spend time with her. Did he think of her as "just a friend"? Did he think of her at all? And what did she think of him, anyhow? As attractive as he was, she wasn't even quite sure how much she liked him.

Nichelle resolved not to let her feelings take over her life. She studied hard, kept up with her fashion column for the *Generation Beat,* and went to the theater with her parents. She even remembered to stop in at the newspaper office and drop off her vote for Andy for student council vice president.

Nichelle knew that a lot of the school had heard about the excitement at Eatz on Tuesday. Everywhere she went, there was a lot of talk about "The Candidate for the Ages," and "Skaters versus Debaters." It was fun, but Nichelle didn't expect anything to come of it.

Was she ever wrong.

On Friday morning, Principal Simmons's voice again came onto the P.A. system. Today, however, everybody knew what she'd be talking about. It was time for the four winning nominees to be announced.

"Good morning, everyone," she began. "I hope you've all had a good week. I'm not going to keep you in suspense, so I'll get right to it. The four students who received the greatest number of nominating votes for student council vice president are: Megan Graham, junior; Max Sklar, senior; Ashley Burt, sophomore; and Andy Groebner, sophomore. Congratulations to these fine candidates."

Andy and Nichelle, sitting across the classroom from each other, exchanged stunned looks. *Andy was in the final running?* Who would have expected it? Nichelle could almost hear him gulp.

"Remember, students," Principal Simmons continued, "to be nominated is a great honor. If, for any reason, any of the candidates do not wish to run, they should see me in my office immediately so that a substitute can be announced. Thank you for your attention. Good luck to all the candidates. Oh, and one last thing. Hurry down to the cafeteria, because today's lunch special will be 'Gourmet Hot Dog Delight.'"

The principal's last few words were hard to hear, however, because almost everyone in homeroom was yelling, "*Duude! Duude!*" in perfect Andy-speak. The kids around him were hammering him on the back and yanking at his hat.

When the bell rang, Nichelle hurried to Andy's side. "Wow, Andy — you won! How do you feel? Do you want to do it?"

"*I d'nno,*" he said. "*S' tot'lly weird, y'know?*"

They turned the corner to see a big knot of kids excitedly crowding around Megan. Among them was one of the debaters, who was saying, "It's in the bag, Megan. You're the only popular one running. The other candidates are so lame. Andy Groebner! Right!"

Someone must have spotted Andy and Nichelle, because there was lots of shush-shushing. Then Thomas stepped out of the group and walked up to Andy. He bowed deeply, in old-movie style, cleared his throat, and said, "Congratulations, my good man. You are indeed 'The Candidate for the Ages.'"

It was clear that Thomas was having trouble keeping a straight face. All his friends were sniggering. Nichelle hadn't expected anything like this.

"I'm sure Andy's on his way down to the office to tell Principal Simmons he's not running," commented another Megan supporter. "Let's not keep him."

Thomas stepped aside. "Too bad it can't go on," he said. "This is so funny. Vice President Skater-Dude! Cracks me up! Well, got to get to class. Thanks for making my morning."

Soon Nichelle and Andy were left standing alone. Nichelle could hardly bring herself to look at her friend's face. When she did, she could see the hurt on it.

"Those debaters are so *arrogant!*" she said angrily. "Why shouldn't a skater be vice president of the student council?"

"*S'right,*" he agreed. "*Why not?*" The stunned, bashful look was now being replaced by an expression Nichelle had never seen on Andy's face. He looked determined. He looked defiant.

"What do you want to do?" she asked him.

"*Nichelle, duude, ahhm runnin'. International High s'for everr'one. Not jus' the hotshots.*"

"You want to run? Are you sure?"

Andy nodded.

"Wow, Andy. That's great. I think you are exactly right; this school belongs to everyone. You'd make an awesome vice president."

The two exchanged a high five before hurrying in opposite directions.

On Saturday morning, Nichelle and Ana took a run together around the reservoir in Central Park. They liked having a chance to catch up and exercise at the same time. Of course, Nichelle ran forward and Ana ran backward in front of her, hardly puffing as they chatted.

"It's been a crazy week," Nichelle said. She told Ana all about Thomas, starting with their trip to the library.

"Would you call that a date?" Nichelle asked. "I don't know if he has a girlfriend — do you? And I'm not even sure how much I like him."

Ana shrugged. "Has he called you or have you seen him since then?"

Nichelle described yesterday's encounter in the hall. "He acted pretty smug. Though, to be fair, I think he thought it was funny. Everyone, even Andy, thought of his nomination as a goof."

"That's true," Ana conceded.

"You should see Andy now though, Ana. He really wants to run. But I don't think he has a chance against Megan, do you?"

"He *is* kinda different," Ana answered. "Why does he want to run?"

"To make a point. The school is for everyone, not just a special few."

"Wow! He's right. He really is smart under all that skater stuff, isn't he?"

"Sure he is. But I don't think he has any idea how to get his message out. I'm afraid the campaign will be very hard on him. He's so shy."

"Do you think he even knows how to run a campaign?" Ana asked.

"Probably not."

"Too bad. You know Megan's going to go all out. Andy needs someone to help him through all this — you know, like a campaign manager."

"But who?" asked Nichelle.

"You know who I'm thinking of?"

"Oh, no!" Nichelle protested.

"C'mon, Nichelle, you know you'd be perfect. Nobody knows the student council better than you. And you have so much energy, and you're so creative."

"I couldn't —"

"Look, you just said you didn't want him to get hurt. I'm sure Megan's group is going to try to make taco meat out of him. There's only one person I know who can protect him."

"You think?" said Nichelle, halting.

"I *know*," said Ana as she jogged in place beside her.

"I guess I could advise him a little. Besides, it would be sweet to teach those hotshots a lesson. I think I *will* ask Andy if he'd like any help."

"You go, girl!" Ana replied, giving Nichelle a big hug.

When she got home, Nichelle called Andy. He answered the phone after just one ring. "*S'Andy. S'upp?*" In the background, she could hear loud screeching sounds. *Parrots, maybe?* thought Nichelle. *Or robots? Clocks?*

Nichelle laid everything out clearly for Andy. His chances. The risks. Then she quickly got to the point. "If you want me to," she offered, "I'll be happy to help you with your campaign."

"*Duude, Nichelle. That'd be phat, man,*" Andy said.

Later that afternoon, Nichelle went to the art supply store in her neighborhood and got lots of poster board and tons of markers and colored pencils.

The next day, Sunday afternoon, Andy, Barbie, Ana, and Lara came over to help her design campaign posters. They all sat down on the kitchen floor.

"Now," Nichelle said, "all we have to do is figure out what to put on the posters."

"What if we give them a distinctive look?" suggested Lara, who was the "art person."

"Like what?" said Ana.

"Well, maybe we could use a clearly identifiable color palette — say, a lot of greens and purples and pinks? And we could use a shape like this . . ." Quickly, she sketched an abstract outline of a skateboard. "Then everybody would recognize Andy's posters right away."

"That's great!" said Nichelle. Everyone else agreed.

"Now, all we have to do is think of something to write on them," said Barbie.

"I already have an idea for that," said Nichelle. She turned to Andy. "I think what you told me the other day — 'I. H. is for everyone' — was such a great thought. It's really the heart of your campaign. So how about if we use something like that?"

"What about 'I. H. Belongs to Us All,'" suggested Barbie.

"*Cool*," said Andy, grinning.

"Great slogan!" said Nichelle. "We've got it."

They went to work in earnest. Lara sketched out the posters and the others filled them in carefully with colored pencils and markers. Even Nichelle's older brother Shawn, who'd strayed into the kitchen looking for a snack, stayed to help out. It was fun, and it was for a good cause. *I. H.* should *belong to us all,* Nichelle thought.

After the group had been working for several hours, Mrs. Williams popped in. "Would you all like to stay for dinner? I'm making chili."

Mrs. Williams's chili was a big favorite with Nichelle's friends, and they all enthusiastically accepted her invitation. After calling their parents to let them know they wouldn't be home for dinner, they moved their operation to the dining room table while Nichelle's mother whipped up supper.

After they'd all eaten lots and lots, they sat around the table in the Williamses' comfortable, warm kitchen and talked about the campaign.

"Do you think you really have a chance?" Mrs. Williams asked.

Campaign Chaos

"With a great candidate like Andy, who's got us — the power team — behind him, we can't lose," said Ana.

"We *will* win!" Nichelle vowed. Everyone in the room cheered.

Chapter 4

Poster Power

On Monday morning, Nichelle suddenly realized that there was no way she could get all the posters to school by herself on the subway. She and Andy had agreed to meet an hour before school started to hang them. The thought of wrestling all this stuff onto the subway at 7 A.M. was more than she could bear.

"I'll tell you what," her dad proposed. "Why don't we all share a cab? You can drop me off at the hospital, and then you and Mom can head downtown. It'll be a special treat."

Nichelle knew that it would cost a fortune, but

she wasn't going to turn down the offer. The posters were a major load to carry.

When she got to school, Nichelle saw that Andy had rounded up lots of kids to help. Their friends Fletcher, Melissa, and Max were in the group, as well as most of her best girlfriends and the entire I. H. skateboarding crew. Some of them were rubbing the sleep out of their eyes, but they all looked enthusiastic.

As they were climbing the steps to go inside, Barbie, who'd already been inside the school, turned to Nichelle and said, "You'd better prepare yourself before you enter."

"What do you mean?"

"She means, mate, that Megan has already got her campaign going great guns," Tori said.

"Well, a few minutes' head start isn't going to make that much difference. Let's not get too excited here. Are you worried, Andy?" Nichelle asked him.

"*Nooo way, Nichelle. S'all okay*," Andy mumbled.

"*S'rite duude*," Evan added, pounding Andy's shoulder.

"Really there is nothing to worry . . ." Nichelle's

words stuck in her throat as she walked into the big entrance hall.

"Oh, my," she finished.

The place looked as if it should have been called "Megan International High School." A huge, professionally made gold banner with *M&M = Megan and Manhattan* splashed across it was strung between the up and down escalators. The *M&M* logo was in the classy-looking shape of a Manhattan skyline. There were mammoth posters everywhere with Megan's photo on them. Loud-speakers were blasting a cool tune with someone rapping about Megan. A table was set up in the middle of the hall, behind which sat kids from the debate club, including Thomas, passing out cookies with big M's formed from M&M candies.

Nearby, Megan was handing out colorful buttons with *M&M* printed on them. She looked really slick, dressed in a beautiful, loose-fitting blue tweed jacket over solid blue capris. When Nichelle looked closer, she saw that the buttons on Megan's jacket looked like M&M candies, too. So did her earrings.

"Ugh! This is just too much," Nichelle said softly as she cast a glance at Andy. He was dressed, as usual, in a stretched-out T-shirt over shorts that hung precariously around his hips. A plaid flannel shirt was tied around his waist by the arms. His grungy hat was stuck backward on his head. And his skateboard protruded from his ripped-up backpack.

"Can you believe this?" Ana asked Nichelle. "It looks more like a governor's race."

"Hey, forget it," Nichelle replied. "We have an election to win. So let's get these posters up."

Nichelle and her friends got to work. Nichelle divided up the posters among groups of kids, and they ran off to stick them up all over the school.

In no time at all they had finished. Nichelle and Andy and Barbie took a walk around the school to check out the results.

"You know, I actually think our posters look better," Barbie said. "They look like real kids did them. They're not as glossy and slick as Megan's. I know everyone will respond to that."

Nichelle noticed that Barbie's remark had made Andy smile — for the first time since they'd walked into school this morning. She gave Barbie an affectionate hug. Barbie always had a positive attitude about things, and it was downright infectious. They were going to need a lot of her sunny optimism if Andy's campaign was ever going to get off the ground.

In fact, Barbie wasn't being overly cheery. The posters really did look good, and there were enough of them to create a real presence. As Lara had intended, they gave Andy's campaign an instantly recognizable look. The other two candidates had only managed to get one or two small notices posted. Perhaps they needed a little more time to gear up. But it was beginning to look as if the real race was going to be between Andy and Megan.

Megan's campaign was the talk of the school for the entire day. Kids were walking along singing the lyrics to the rap song. Nichelle saw those *M&M* buttons everywhere.

At lunch, Nichelle sat with Barbie, Ana, and Chelsie. Chelsie was still worrying about her lost book, and her friends were trying as best they could to reassure her. But Nichelle was only half there. At the next table, two girls from the debate club talked as they picked at their "Goulash Italiana." Nichelle could not help overhearing their conversation.

"Thomas is doing such a great job on Megan's campaign," said one.

"Well, what would you expect? They've gotten back together again."

"That's not what I heard," the first girl replied. "I heard he still feels it's over, and that he's only doing it because of the skater-debater thing. Rick made him do it."

"Well, even if they're not back yet," the second girl said knowingly, "I bet they will be by the election. Megan's no dope. She knows she's going to have a lot of time alone with him. I bet she'll make her move fast."

A chill went through Nichelle. Did she hear correctly? Were the debaters saying that Thomas and Megan were possibly an item, and that Thomas was now managing her campaign? Too stunned to eat, Nichelle said good-bye to her friends and walked out of the cafeteria toward her locker.

She began to have weird, unsettling thoughts. Had Thomas taken charge of Megan's campaign in order to spite Nichelle and her friends? Had Thomas and Megan, in fact, gotten back together? It was news to Nichelle that they'd ever been close in the first place. And if they weren't an item, as the second debater had maintained, had Nichelle blown her chances with him now that they were handling rival political campaigns? Nichelle took a series of deep cleansing breaths that gradually calmed her down. It's important not to jump to conclusions, she told herself. There was absolutely no way Thomas could have known that she was managing Andy's campaign. So Thomas wasn't doing anything to get back at her. Besides, she hadn't cleared her decision with him. Why should he feel obliged to clear his with her?

As to why he hadn't called her since their "date" last week, why, he'd probably been so busy organizing Megan's campaign that he didn't have time to call. That explained it. Didn't it?

When Nichelle got home late that afternoon there were two messages waiting for her, both in Shawn's scrawled handwriting. The first said, *Call Chelsie. Important.* On the second, Shawn had written, *Sis, the modeling agency called. They have you set up for a shoot at Michael Morse's studio for tomorrow at 3 P.M. 745 W. 21st St. Call Sue to confirm.* The note was signed with a huge S.

Wow! Michael Morse. One of the best-known fashion photographers in the city. This would be good — maybe designer clothes. Nichelle hurried to call Sue, her agent, back.

"I'm sorry about the short notice," Sue said. "But Morse sometimes operates like that. Calls right out of the blue." She paused. "Can you do it?"

"You know I can!" replied Nichelle.

"At three, then?" Sue asked.

"Three is perf —"

"— Great! Bye!" said Sue.

Next Nichelle dialed M'dear, her grandmother. By law, Nichelle had to be accompanied by an adult on her photo shoots, and M'dear, who really was a dear, usually went along with her.

"Hi!" said Nichelle when her grandmother picked up the phone. She knew she wouldn't need to tell M'dear who was calling; M'dear recognized her voice instantly.

"We've got a big-deal job tomorrow," Nichelle informed her. "Michael Morse. Fancy-dancy photographer! I know it's short notice, but can you come with me at three?"

"Let me just look at my calendar," said M'dear. "Aha. Tuesday? You're in luck. My book group meets at noon, but I'm sure we'll be done by then. Just tell me where to go, and I'll be there."

Nichelle gave her the address, sent her a noisy smooch, and said good-bye.

Now it was time to call Chelsie. Nichelle knew if the message said "Important," it was probably something about her lost book.

"Oh, Nichelle, I'm so glad you've called!" said Chelsie in her well-bred British accent.

"What's the word?"

"Well, I followed your advice, and I actually found out that there is such a thing as a Taxi and Limousine Commission. So I went there directly after school today. The neighborhood was a bit dodgy, I can tell you — my mother would have had a fit if she'd seen me there! But, anyway, guess what? They have a computer there with the home phone numbers of all the cab drivers in it!"

"So, did you get a number for your cab driver?"

"Well, not exactly. The lady said she couldn't give it to me. She wasn't very pleasant, I must say. But she did agree to get in touch with him for me. She asked me for my phone number, so he could ring me back, and I just *froze*. What if he called and my mum answered? So . . . I gave her your number. I hope you don't mind."

"No, I don't mind at all. If he calls, I'll call you right away."

"Oh, I hope he does! And I hope he found the book in his cab. I'm so afraid that it fell out onto the street. I'd never be able to face my mum again! It would break her heart if she knew."

"Let's hope for the best," Nichelle reassured her.

When she was off the phone, Nichelle wondered what would be "the best" in her own situation. Dating Thomas, the mastermind of the enemy's political campaign? Was she crazy enough to do that? *Oh, dear,* she thought. *Life would be so much easier if it weren't for Thomas.*

Less interesting, though.

Chapter 5

Magic by Monique

"**A**nd so you see, The Kansas and Nebraska Act was pivotal . . ." Mr. Budge droned on. Nichelle's thoughts were miles away. About two miles, in fact. At Michael Morse's photography studio. She knew that the shoot this afternoon could be very important for her career. And she couldn't believe the day she was having. It had been pouring all morning. Her hair had declared war. There was all the election stuff. Two pop quizzes. Plus a surprise *Generation Beat* meeting, so she'd had about ten minutes to eat today's awful cafeteria food ("Sausages on Toast, à la Swiss"). The list went on. On a different day, she might have gone home for a nap before starting her homework. Today, it was off to the most important assignment in her modeling life. That is, if the bell would ever ring.

Brring! At last. It was like the start of a race as kids sprinted for the door. Nichelle didn't even take the time to sling her silver backpack over her shoulder — she just carried it in her hand as she rushed to her locker. She grabbed her coat and ran down the steps. There was no time to walk to the subway — she'd have to take a cab.

Megan Graham was out front with some of her friends. "Hey, Nichelle," one of them called back to her, "I hear your 'Candidate for the Ages' really blew it today before seventh period. Busted by Mr. Merlin for skateboarding in the hall. Great example he's setting."

"Gossip has no place in this campaign," Nichelle responded, and kept going. This was the first she'd heard about this. Was it true? She had no idea. She hailed a cab, fell into the back seat, and gave the driver Michael Morse's address. All the way there she did her deep breathing exercises. *Calm and centered, calm and centered*, she kept saying to herself.

M'dear was waiting outside the studio when

Nichelle ran up the stairs to the second floor. "There you are, sweetheart," she said to her granddaughter. "Don't run, you still have time to spare."

"What a day!" Nichelle said as she bent to give her grandmother a kiss. She had to bend a lot, since M'dear was about nine inches shorter than she was. "Thank you so much for coming on short notice. I wouldn't have been able to take this job if it weren't for you."

"You know I love doing this," replied M'dear.

As soon as Nichelle and M'dear entered the studio, a slight young woman with long, very straight red hair came springing forward. She was wearing big black shoes and a floaty chartreuse nylon smock over her chic black clothes. There was a name embroidered on the smock, but Nichelle didn't need to read it. She recognized the woman on sight as Monique Dutou, the famous makeup artist. Nichelle even had some of the "Monique" line of cosmetics on her dressing table at home. Was it possible that Monique Dutou herself would be doing Nichelle's makeup today?

So it appeared. After stopping in front of Nichelle and looking her over, Monique did an about-face and crooked her finger, indicating that

Nichelle should follow. They headed to a corner where tables covered with jars and bottles of cosmetics and lots and lots of brushes had been set up. "Sit, please," Monique said in a French accent, indicating one of the tall director's chairs. "We have a lot to do. I am going to work on your hair, too, so we do not need a hairstylist today."

She frowned as she looked closely at Nichelle's face. "You look a bit tired today, *ma chéri*. Don't worry. Close your eyes. Monique will fix."

Nichelle closed her eyes. She could feel Monique applying a warm cloth to her skin. It smelled minty and it tingled. Nichelle began to relax. Next, she felt Monique deftly applying some kind of cream. This was followed by swipes with various brushes to her cheeks, eyelids, and lips. Monique worked more quickly and surely than any makeup artist Nichelle had ever encountered, all the while singing to herself in French. In the background Nichelle could hear the photographer's assistants setting up lights and props for the shoot. She wasn't nervous at all. She felt calm, totally clear-minded. No, she felt more — she felt like she was now in heaven.

In this blissful state, Nichelle's thoughts drifted over to Andy and his campaign. Andy was just as worthy a candidate as Megan, she reflected. He wasn't just a 'boarder, as Megan's group was trying to make kids believe. He was just, well, a little unconventional. How could she get kids to look past appearances and see Andy for the smart, caring person he was?

Monique spoke, startling her. "Open the eyes and look into the mirror," she commanded.

Nichelle couldn't believe what she saw. What a transformation! Where was the tired girl who'd sat down in the chair just minutes ago?

"You have had a makeover, no?" said Monique, smiling.

"An amazing makeover," Nichelle replied, smiling back. Then it hit her. *Makeover? Of course! That's what we need to do. We need to change the outer Andy so that the inner Andy can shine through.* All it would take would be the right clothes, a few lessons in self-assertion, and a good, clear message. Then nobody would doubt his credibility as a candidate. Nichelle was so excited that she let out a little yell.

Monique, who had now turned to Nichelle's hair, looked up, concerned. "Have I hurt you, *chéri?*" she asked.

"Oh no! In fact, you've just given me a really great idea."

Monique gave her a quizzical look, shrugged, and continued combing.

At last, it was time to start working. Nichelle walked out onto the studio floor, where Michael Morse was waiting.

"A pleasure to be working with you," he said to her. "I think you're really going places. We all expect big things from you."

"Thank you!" replied Nichelle, trying not to faint.

The shoot went smoothly; the photographer, like Monique, really knew what he was doing, and it showed. He treated Nichelle and everyone else on the shoot in the most cordial and professional way, and even took the time to offer M'dear coffee while she waited. The stylist moved quietly about, arranging the clothing and props till everything was just right. The background music was Charlie Parker, one of Nichelle's favorite jazz musicians. And the clothes were wonderful. The best was a dress with a huge, full, kelly green taffeta skirt that looked like something Cinderella might have worn to the ball.

By the time she and M'dear left, Nichelle was walking on air. "That was a lot better than the last shoot I had for that catalog!" she said to her grandmother.

"I remember that one," M'dear agreed. "Not nearly as pleasant."

At dinner Nichelle described the shoot to her family.

"It's easy to see how much modeling means to you," her dad said.

Nichelle loved to hear this, because for a time her parents had not been enthusiastic about her chosen career.

"I do love modeling. It's creative work. You know, I think I learned to love it right here at home, playing dress-up with all those great old clothes in the attic." Nichelle's mother's family had lived in this house for generations, and the small attic was stuffed with old treasures. Even when her parents had had the house renovated, the attic was left untouched.

"It's too bad you didn't get to keep that green dress you wore today," said her mother.

"Only in my dreams," agreed Nichelle.

Then she told her parents about her brainstorm regarding Andy. "All he needs is a little Cinder-Andy makeover," she said excitedly. "Do you think it might work?"

Mrs. Williams frowned. "It's a good idea in principle," she said. "But you're already so busy, Nichelle. I don't want this campaign to take time away from your schoolwork."

"I won't be doing it alone," Nichelle replied. "My friends will help."

"They'll have to," Shawn blurted. "Andy's got a long, long way to go before he'll look like a real candidate. Let alone a 'Candidate for the Ages.'"

Nichelle shot her brother a look. "You have to look beyond the exterior with some people, you know."

"You should apply that lesson to yourself, sis," Shawn retorted.

"What do you mean?"

"I mean Mr. Thomas 'The Man' Garie. Don't go and get yourself hurt. Besides, I'm not saying that Andy won't be a good student council veep. Just that he's got to change a whole lot before he can get the votes he needs. Count me in if you need help."

"Honest? Thanks." This vote of confidence from

her older brother meant a lot to Nichelle. But what did he mean about Thomas?

The conversation at the dinner table changed course as Shawn told his family about a water main break that had flooded the library of the city's public dramatic arts high school. All of the school's books were ruined. He thought that maybe I. H. students could do something to help the other school. Nichelle tried to help her brother come up with some ideas, but her mind just kept turning back to the election.

After dinner, Nichelle went up to her room. It was time to launch "Operation Cinder-Andy." First she called Barbie, who was the best public speaker she knew. "Do you think you could maybe give Andy some speech lessons?" she asked.

"Of course," Barbie replied. "I could even lend him some of the elocution tapes I use for acting."

"That would be wonderful, Barbie. Thanks."

Next she called Tori.

"I need you to set up an Internet website for Andy's campaign," Nichelle said. "Somewhere kids can go to read Andy's views about school issues.

Maybe they should also be able to E-mail him questions that he can answer on-line."

"That's an ace idea," the Australian exclaimed. "It avoids the mumble problem."

"Exactly," said Nichelle.

"When do you need it?" Tori asked.

Nichelle bit her lip. "By, um, tomorrow after-noon, if possible?"

A loud gulp came across the line. After a short pause, Tori spoke. "Crikey, Nichelle, you don't ask for much, do you?"

"I know it's a lot. But can you do it?" she asked hopefully.

"For Andy — anything. I'll call Lara and get her working on the graphics tonight. That'll save time. It'll be a bonzer website! *Ask Andy On-line*."

"Excellent."

Nichelle and Tori chatted for a few more min-utes, working out the details of the website, then said good-bye. Immediately, the phone rang again.

"Hallo?" said a man's voice.

"Yes?" said Nichelle a bit warily. "Who's this?"

"Muhammad Ali. I get phone call about book. Red book. Poems."

"Oh!" said Nichelle. "The cab driver!"

"Cab driver, right."

"Can we pick it up from you?" Nichelle asked excitedly.

"No," said the man. Nichelle's heart sank.

"Henry Chu has it," he said.

"Henry Chu?" she echoed, bewildered.

"Yes. He shares cab with me. He drives day shift. He found book under seat. Shows me later."

"Oh, that's wonderful!" said Nichelle. "How do we find him?"

Mr. Ali gave Nichelle an address on Mott Street, in Chinatown. "Henry goes home at two. Then I get cab," he said.

Nichelle thanked him profusely, said good-bye, and instantly called Chelsie.

"Chelsie!" she said. "Guess what? He called!"

"Who called?"

"Your cab driver! He knows where the book is!"

Chelsie let out a shriek of joy. "How absolutely fabulous!" she cried. "Nichelle, you're a wonder! Can we go get it?"

Nichelle explained about Henry Chu and gave Chelsie the address.

"Will you go to Chinatown with me tomorrow

after school?" Chelsie begged. "I don't know that neighborhood at all."

Nichelle couldn't say no. "Sure," she replied. "If we can do it fast."

The conversation then turned to Nichelle's big idea. "So, will you join the Andy Makeover Machine?" she asked.

"Of course," Chelsie answered.

They finished by talking about the shoot at Michael Morse's studio.

"You're on your way, kid," Chelsie said in a silly deep voice.

"I'm on my way to trouble if I don't get going on my homework. I'll see you tomorrow."

Nichelle finished up her homework and got ready to snuggle under her cozy, purple down comforter with a fashion magazine. Relaxation time.

And then the phone rang again. With a sigh, Nichelle reached over to her bedside table to get it. She hoped it was for Shawn this time.

"Hi, Nichelle. It's Thomas," said that deep, thrilling voice. He was the last person she expected to be calling her. Immediately, she found herself in the same confused state as she always found herself in whenever she talked to him.

"Listen," he said. "I have to go back to the library tomorrow and do some research for an English paper. Do you want to come along?"

"Well," she said, "I do have an English paper due next week. I could do some work on it there. Sure, I'll come along."

"Maybe we could grab some dinner afterward?"

"Okay," she said hesitantly.

"Meet me after school?"

She suddenly remembered about Henry Chu. "I have an errand to run right after school," she said. "Can I meet you at the library around four?" That would give her enough time to get there.

"Great," he said. "I'll meet you in the reading room. Four o'clock."

They said good-bye.

Of course, after the call from Thomas there was no chance of her relaxing with a magazine. Her mind was too busy wondering why Thomas made her feel so flustered.

That night Nichelle dreamed that I. H. had become a big carnival. Mr. Budge was walking around selling cotton candy. The escalators had turned into Ferris wheels. In the middle of the hall was an arcade game covered in flashing lights.

68

Music was blasting from it. Instead of a row of ducks to knock down, there were tiny mechanical skateboarders, all resembling Andy. Standing at the counter, surrounded by a crowd of debaters and friends, was Megan, wearing the beautiful green dress Nichelle had modeled at Michael Morse's. She was holding a baseball in her hand and looked menacing as the mob chanted, "We rule the school."

Each time Megan threw, a new baseball appeared magically in her hand. The first throw was wild. But the following ones got closer and closer. Suddenly, the little mechanical skateboarders came to life. They ducked her pitches and shouted back at the crowd, "I. H. is for us all!" in robot-like voices.

Nichelle saw herself in the dream, too. She was standing to one side in her pajamas. She wasn't sure whether anyone could see her or not. She wanted to yell, "I. H. is for everyone," but she couldn't speak.

Chapter 6

"Cinder-Andy"

On Wednesday morning, Nichelle was up even before her alarm went off. There was so much to do. First, she had to decide what to wear. She knew she wouldn't have time to change before meeting Thomas. After trying on capris, she decided on a black knit dress with three-quarter length sleeves. With Thomas, the more sophisticated, the better, she thought.

Next, she needed to pull together a respectable outfit for Andy. Figuring that Shawn and Andy were about the same size, she woke her brother and asked him to donate a gray oxford cloth shirt and his awesome-looking green tweed suit to the cause.

She completed the look with two "power" ties, courtesy of her dad. That done, she called Andy and asked him to meet her at lunch to talk campaign strategy. She could barely hear him above that strange squawking noise in the background again.

Last on her list was a quick call to Barbie. "I need your help when I talk to Andy at lunch," Nichelle said. "I haven't told him about the makeover yet. I'm worried he'll be offended. I think Andy trusts you. If you're there, it'll help soften the shock."

"I'm there," Barbie said simply.

"I knew I could count on you," replied Nichelle. "With the election in two days, we don't have any time to lose."

At lunchtime, Nichelle, Barbie, and Andy huddled together in the far corner of the school cafeteria. Andy's eyes lit up when Nichelle told him about the web page Tori and Lara were creating.

"*S'totally awsum,*" he said, and immediately dashed off five excellent ideas to cover on the page: community-service incentives; a student-sponsored antismoking campaign; a scholarship fund for study abroad; a "lend-a-hand club" aimed at helping struggling students with course work; and an annual student council–run workshop on "How to Get into the College of Your Dreams." Then, while Nichelle and Barbie sat there open-mouthed, Andy quickly composed five logical, beautifully written paragraphs explaining his positions on each of these issues.

Nichelle read them over and smiled. "This is perfect, Andy," she said. "I didn't know you were such a good writer."

"*T's a secret,*" he said, blushing.

"I'll pass this on to Tori," Nichelle continued. "It'll be on your web page before school ends today. Anybody who reads it can see how much you care about the school." Then Nichelle took a deep breath and looked at Barbie. It was time to talk makeover.

Initially, Andy didn't warm to the idea. Then Barbie explained to him that they weren't proposing that Andy change his personality — or his message — one bit. They were only suggesting that he change his look, just a little, and only for two days.

"It'll catch the opposition unawares," Barbie

said, "and it'll take away one of their big issues — that you aren't a 'serious' contender."

Andy turned to Nichelle. "*Y'really think s'necessary?*" he asked.

Nichelle nodded.

"*Okaay, duudes. If 'ats what it takes. I got th' juice. Les go for it.*"

"Yess!" cried Nichelle. "Let the transformation begin. On to the band room!"

Nichelle led the way down the hall to an empty band practice room, where she had stashed Andy's campaign wear. The makeover team got right to work. What a difference the clothes made. Andy looked great in the suit. Nichelle thought he would have looked even better with a haircut, but she didn't want to push him too far.

"The debate on Friday will be crucial," Nichelle told Andy as she ran a comb through his unruly hair. "That's where everybody will get a chance to, uh, hear your ideas. Now, you really have some great ideas. It's just that . . ." Nichelle paused. She really didn't know how to tell Andy that he would also have to change the way he talked if he was to be understood.

Barbie jumped in to help. "Andy," she began, "remember when we first met you? How only Lara could —"

Andy burst out laughing. "*S'matter, duude? Say it. I need help with public speakin'. Ahh know that.*"

"You're only slightly unintelligible," Nichelle laughed.

"*Not t' Evan,*" grinned Andy.

Barbie laughed and gave him a hug. "You'll be great," she said. "I've been studying speech for years. Believe me, it isn't so hard to learn how to speak clearly."

"And you can go back to talking your regular way after the debate's over," said Nichelle, "if this hurts your mouth."

Barbie now gripped Andy's shoulders. "Let's start with your posture. Stand up straight. That'll dramatically improve your voice projection."

Andy straightened his shoulders and lifted his chest.

"Perfect," said Barbie. Next, she got him to hold a pencil between his teeth and repeat, "My mother makes me muffins."

At first, Andy's pronunciation sounded like a man trying to gargle with his lips closed. After several repetitions, though, his words became clearer. Everyone agreed that he still had a long way to go. But Andy was making amazing progress.

Suddenly, Ana rushed into the room. "You won't believe this," she said. "Megan had a bakery make up hundreds of jumbo cookies with her picture on them in fancy-colored frosting. She's going to give them away on the day of the debate."

"You can't buy votes with cookies," remarked Barbie.

"Still, we've got to find a way to top them," Nichelle said. "But what? Think, guys!"

The group spent the next few minutes brainstorming.

"We don't want to be super-slick," Ana said.

"Right," agreed Nichelle.

"We should play to our strengths," threw in Barbie.

"But what are our strengths?" queried Ana.

"That's obvious," replied Nichelle. "We're different, yet sincere."

"*And,*" Andy interjected, "*We're not jus' for the few, we're for everr' one.*"

"Andy's web page will help get our message across," Nichelle added.

"I agree," Ana said. "But how is everyone going to know about it?"

"Well, um —" Nichelle said, fumbling. Then a gleam came into her eyes. "I've got it. We'll just have to get everyone talking about it."

"How?" asked Ana.

Nichelle grinned. "By fighting cookies with sticky notes."

"Huh?" everybody asked.

"It's simple," Nichelle explained. "We'll get some rubber stamps made with Andy's name and web page address on them. Then we'll stamp lots and lots of brightly colored sticky notes and put them up all over the school. In phone booths, on lockers, on lunch trays, on bulletin boards, on clocks in the hallway, on mirrors in the bathrooms. Wherever kids turn, they'll see a sticky note. By tomorrow, there won't be a single kid in the school who won't know Andy's name or web page address."

"You're a genius, Ms. Williams!" Ana cried. And spontaneously, everyone broke into applause.

Barbie volunteered to get the stamps made on her way home, and Ana and Andy agreed to come to Barbie's apartment later and start mass-producing sticky notes.

"Thanks, everyone," Nichelle called as she headed down the hall toward her English class. "Megan's group won't know what hit them. That's the way the cookie crumbles!"

It wasn't until sixth-period English, when Mrs. Hong spent the opening minutes of the class refining the requirements for the paper due next week, that Nichelle remembered her date with Thomas. How weird it was, she thought, to have to switch from being Thomas's date one moment to being his political nemesis the next. Well, she supposed, if it didn't bother him, it probably shouldn't bother her.

She gazed fitfully at the clock. Just one more period left. In roughly one hour she'd be heading over to Chinatown with Chelsie. Then she'd go racing uptown to meet Thomas at the library. *What a life!* she thought.

Emerging from the subway in Chinatown, Nichelle and Chelsie started walking across Canal Street toward Henry Chu's address. Every step of the way they saw something that captured their attention. They stopped at one stand to marvel at the colorful array of fresh fruits and vegetables.

Neat stacks of bright green bok choy, a big tangled pile of extra long green beans, pyramids of shiny oranges. In one corner were piles of round, pale-gold fruits. An old man arranging the fruits noticed the girls' interest and cut one of them into wedges. With a smile, he offered the slices to Nichelle and Chelsie. They were delicious. Nichelle had never tasted anything like it before. The fruit had the crunch of a fresh apple and the delicate sweetness of a pear. "They're called Asian pears," the man told them.

Next door, the girls spent a few minutes admiring the merchant's stock of delicately embroidered clothing. Nichelle, with her keen eye for fashion, could really appreciate how much work had gone into each stitched pastel flower.

At last, they reached Mr. Chu's address. It was up two narrow flights of wooden stairs, above a busy restaurant.

Chelsie knocked loudly. Soon a slight, baggy-eyed man appeared at the door.

"Mr. Chu?" Chelsie inquired.

"Yes," said the man with a yawn.

"My name is Chelsie. This is my friend Nichelle. We're students at International High."

"What can I do for you?" asked Mr. Chu.

"I was told by Mr. Ali that you found my book."

"Oh, yes. Poems. By Blake."

Chelsie jumped for joy. "I've come to pick it up."

"I am so sorry, Miss," the man said, rubbing his eyes. "But I no longer have it."

"B-but you have to!" Chelsie stammered. "Mr. Ali said — "

"Please, let me explain," Mr. Chu interrupted. "I drive nights and sleep afterward. I gave your book to my girlfriend. She put the book in her purse for safekeeping. Then she forgot and took the book home. The book is not lost, don't worry. My girlfriend is keeping it safe."

Chelsie looked distraught. "How can I find your girlfriend?"

Mr. Chu fished a scrap of paper from his pocket. "Her name is Maria Fuentes. Call her at this number. Everything will turn out okay." Then the thin gentleman backed slowly into his apartment. "I am so sorry, Miss. But I have to return to sleep. I must start driving at midnight." With that, he gave them a smile and closed the door.

Chelsie stared at the number in her hand.

On their way back to the subway, Nichelle tried

to cheer her friend up. "Well, I guess you could say that your book is getting a grand tour of New York," she said.

"Quite," replied Chelsie in terse British fashion.

"You know, if you can wait until tomorrow," Nichelle continued, "I'll go with you to see Maria Fuentes," she offered.

"Thanks," Chelsie said, brightening. "I'll take you up on that. I seem to be leaning on you lately like a big sister."

"Hey, what are sisters for, anyway?" replied Nichelle with a smile.

At the subway station, the two friends caught an express train going up the East Side. Nichelle hopped off at Forty-second Street, while Chelsie continued on.

It was a cool, clear afternoon. Noting that she had a few minutes to spare, Nichelle decided to walk the short distance to the library at Fifth Avenue.

Chapter 7

The Dating Game

Even in the packed main reading room, Nichelle was able to pick Thomas out from the crowd. He was sitting near the information desk, wearing a tapered blue shirt and a tie. Draped over his chair was a stylish blue blazer. He didn't slouch in his seat as so many others did. He had presence. Everything about him said *smart, confident, alert.*

Thomas looked up, seeming to sense Nichelle's eyes upon him. He flashed her a huge smile and beckoned her over. "Don't you look nice," he said, rising and pulling a chair out for her.

Bubbles exploded in Nichelle's head. Her arms

and legs felt rubbery, seemingly operating on their own. "Hi," she forced herself to say as she took her seat. "Thanks. You, too . . . I mean, it's nice to see you, Thomas." Her mouth was as dry as sand.

"Did you bring work?" he asked.

"About two tons. How about you?"

He laughed easily, as if she'd just said the cleverest thing. "Maybe only about a ton and a half."

Nichelle grinned back. Would she ever be able to get any work done with him sitting so close? she wondered. But, in fact, it proved surprisingly easy. Thomas set a good example by quickly turning to his books. In no time, Nichelle found herself absorbed in reading two required essays for her English paper.

When she'd finished that, Nichelle reached for her silver backpack to fetch her history textbook.

Noticing the book, Thomas leaned over and threw his arm around the back of Nichelle's chair. "What are you covering now?" he asked.

There was that cologne again. Now just breathing took all of Nichelle's effort. "Ahh . . . you know . . . ahh . . . Civil War battles."

Thomas put his hand on her arm and squeezed. "You have my sympathy. Budge is a real Civil War nut. He can't understand why everyone isn't as crazy about battles and artillery as he is, right?"

Nichelle nodded mutely. Her arm felt so nice and warm where his fingers were closed around it.

"You know," Thomas said, "we've been here about two hours. I think we deserve a break. Would dinner at La Petite Maison be all right?"

"Sounds lovely."

"Let's go then," Thomas said. He helped Nichelle with her coat.

The restaurant was perfect. Nichelle was glad that she'd decided on the black dress, because everyone in the place was dressed up. The maître d' led them to a small table in a cozy corner of the room. As they sat down, he handed them large menus written in French.

Nichelle looked around. The walls weren't painted — they were covered with red-and-white peppermint-striped cloth. The same cloth was gathered in huge billowy bunches at the windows. In the center of each linen-covered table was a tiny lantern and a vase containing a spray of perfect white orchids. So romantic.

The menu was a problem, though. Nichelle was a fairly sophisticated eater, but this menu had dishes she'd never heard of. *Ris de veau. Tournedos.* What was this stuff?

Thomas instantly put her at ease. "Do you mind if I order?" he asked. "There are a few house specialties they don't list on the menu. And I'd love you to try some."

"That would be great," Nichelle answered.

When the waiter appeared, Thomas ordered in fluent French. Minutes later, the waiter returned with steaming crocks of onion soup.

"Be careful, Nichelle," Thomas cautioned. "These just came out of the oven."

Under a crust of bread topped with bubbling cheese, the soup itself was rich and sweet. Nichelle enjoyed every delicious bite. The next course was equally wonderful: tender chicken breasts in lemon sauce, served on a huge blue china plate. On the side, she had a mound of crispy, matchstick-sized french fries and a dish of tiny green beans.

As they ate, they talked about school and about Thomas's plans for next year. "I want to go to an Ivy League school because I'm interested in a career in politics," he said. "The Ivies are the gateway to politics, you know. What about you, modeling or college?"

"I hope to do both. But I'll drop the modeling if it interferes with my education. School is very important to me."

The conversation drifted around. They talked about New York, about sports, about the weather. It was all very pleasant.

Next, they had a green salad with chopped olives sprinkled over it. "In France the salad usually follows the main course," Thomas informed her.

Following the salad, they had dark chocolate mousse. As they were eating the creamy dessert, Thomas began to talk about the school election.

"You know, Nichelle, you and I are a lot alike. We're both hard workers and high achievers. I know I've been working hard on Megan's campaign. And I'm sure you've been working hard for Andy."

Nichelle nodded slowly. What was Thomas getting at?

"In many ways, politics is like a game," he went on. "I move here, you move there. We chase each other around the board."

"Right," said Nichelle warily.

"I guess you heard about our secret cookie surprise. One of the sophomores on the debate team couldn't keep his mouth shut. Now it's all over school."

Nichelle took a sip of water and smiled. "Yes, I did hear something about that."

Thomas smiled back. "Knowing you, I bet you've come up with a few surprises for Friday, too, right?"

All kinds of warning sirens went off in Nichelle's head. "Maybe I have, and maybe I haven't," she said. The smile on her face was rapidly disappearing.

"You know, Nichelle, I really like you," Thomas said. "And I would hate to see you embarrass yourself over this silly election. You really have a challenge with your candidate."

Nichelle felt a spike of anger. She didn't like Thomas's patronizing tone. "Let's talk about something else," she suggested.

"Just hear me out," Thomas went on. "I've got a proposal I think you might like."

"I'm listening."

"Well, ever since I heard you had become Andy's campaign manager, I've been asking myself, 'How can I help Nichelle make the best of a lost cause?'

Then it came to me. Since we all know Megan's going to win, maybe I could help you refine your campaign strategy so that Andy comes in a strong second."

Nichelle couldn't believe her ears. "Are you asking me to tell you the confidential advice I've been giving Andy?"

"I wouldn't put it quite that way," Thomas said. "I'm only suggesting that you might want to let me help you save Andy from a humiliating defeat."

Nichelle was furious. She stood up and threw her napkin down on her plate. "Thanks for your concern, Thomas," she said, "but no thanks."

"Be reasonable," Thomas said, looking around uneasily as several startled diners stared over at their table.

"You know, I may only be a sophomore," Nichelle snapped, "but I can take care of myself. And I also happen to believe that Andy has something new to offer the school. You ask if we've got any surprises planned? Well, I'll tell you. We do. And the biggest one will be the election results on Friday, when Andy wins."

"Please, Nichelle. Don't make a scene."

Nichelle gathered her things together. "It's time I got home, Thomas," she said, leaving. "Thank you for an interesting evening."

When Nichelle entered the house, she found her mom at the kitchen table, paying bills. Her mother took one look at her face and guessed what had happened. "Not a big success, huh?" she said, rising and giving Nichelle a hug.

"Not even close," Nichelle replied with a weak smile, sinking down into a straight-backed chair. Then, as her mother made tea, she kicked off her shoes and related the whole sad story of her "date" with Thomas.

"Yep, that's pretty bad," her mother agreed.

"Are all boys such big pains?" Nichelle asked.

"Hardly. Look at your dad and your brother."

"Okay," said Nichelle with a pouty grin. "Maybe I'll give you two."

Her mother laughed. "That's my girl," she said. "You know, sometimes the best ones aren't the ones with all that flash, but the ones who grow on you steadily."

"I know," Nichelle said. "But why couldn't the cute ones — just for once — be the nice kind, too?"

Nichelle and her mom stayed up after everyone else had gone to bed and talked and talked. Finally, Mrs. Williams stole a look at the clock. "You'd better get some sleep now," she said. "You can't help Andy if you're running on empty."

"Oh, gosh — thanks for reminding me," Nichelle said. "I just have to make one quick phone call, then it's off to dreamland."

She dialed Andy's number. He answered the phone after one ring. "*S'Andy. S'upp?*"

There was that strange shrieking sound in the background again. What could it possibly be?

"Hi, Andy. How's it going?"

"*Th' bes', Nichelle. Have I gotta suprise f' you.*"

"A surprise? What is it?"

"*Noo way, duude. You jus' have to wait.*"

"That's what I called about," Nichelle said. "Will you be able to get to the band room early tomorrow — before school?"

"*Noo problem, duude.*"

"Great. See you then."

A surprise? Nichelle wasn't sure she needed any more of them.

Chapter 8

The Campaign Heats Up

Early Thursday morning, an hour before school started, Nichelle, Barbie, Ana, Tori, Lara, and Chelsie rendezvoused in the band room. Evan, Fletcher, Melissa, and about a dozen other volunteers were already fanning out over the school, putting up the sticky notes that Ana, Barbie, and Andy had made the night before. Tori and Lara reported that Andy's web page was up and running. And thanks to a small notice that Tori had posted on the *Generation Beat* website yesterday, it had already been visited by more than four hundred students — about one out of every ten voters.

Campaign Chaos

Everything was going off like clockwork. There was only one problem: Where was their candidate?

To save time, Barbie set up a tape recorder with her elocution tapes. "I bet he's just running a little late," she offered.

"Was that a pun?" Nichelle asked.

Just then, the door swung open and Andy walked in. He was wearing his usual droopy shorts, grungy T-shirt, and baseball cap. But as soon as the door closed, he yanked off his hat and spread his arms wide, like a performer inviting applause.

"I can't believe it!" cried Ana.

"This is historic," remarked Tori, gaping.

Everyone else nodded in agreement. Andy had indeed done something major. He'd gotten a *haircut*! Gone were his spiky tufts. In their place were natural pale-brown locks trimmed into a neat, almost executive-style cut. What a difference!

Nichelle felt a surge of admiration for her friend. She knew how hard it must have been for Andy to do this. "You really do want to win, don't you?" she said.

Andy grinned and raised his fingers in the "V for Victory" sign.

"Is this the surprise you were talking about?" Nichelle asked.

Andy smiled and said, "*Y'll hafta wait an' see.*"

The group wasted no time getting things underway. Barbie and Andy went over his speaking exercises. "My mother makes me muffins" was sounding surprisingly better. "If wishes were horses" and several other drills still needed some work, though.

"Whenever you focus, you speak clearly," Barbie said. "So focus, focus, focus."

Meanwhile Lara, Ana, and Chelsie huddled with Nichelle, talking strategy. "There's only one explanation for Thomas's actions last night," Nichelle said. "Megan's people must be feeling a little less confident than they did a week ago."

"I agree," Chelsie said. "I got a call last night from a reliable source in the senior class. He said that Rick had taken a poll on Tuesday and found that Max Sklar was cutting heavily into Megan's junior and senior vote while Andy was carrying freshmen and sophomores by a five-to-one margin."

"This is meaning what?" asked Lara in her adorable French accent.

"It means," Nichelle explained, "that if Rick's numbers are anywhere near accurate, our candidate is . . . the FRONTRUNNER!"

Lara, Ana, Chelsie, and Nichelle let out a whoop that startled Andy so much that he nearly bit through the pencil in his mouth. When Nichelle repeated the good news for Barbie and Andy, they whooped for joy, too.

When it came time for the meeting to end, Andy tucked his hair back under his familiar cap. Then, as everyone headed off to homeroom together, Nichelle announced, "Remember, guys, win or lose, there'll be a party at my house on Friday night after the election."

As the day unfolded, it became clearer to Nichelle that her sticky-note campaign had created a huge buzz in the school. Dozens of students came up to her and congratulated her on how clever it was. Others said that it had prompted them to visit Andy's web page during lunch or one of their free periods. Some went even further. They said they'd been so impressed by Andy's ideas that they'd decided to switch their votes from Megan to Andy. The final testament to Nichelle's success was the parade of scowls she received from Megan's supporters as they passed her in the halls.

After seventh period, a jubilant Nichelle met

Chelsie at her locker and told her about her experiences.

"It really looks like the tide is shifting in our favor," Chelsie said.

"Let's not get overconfident," Nichelle cautioned. "There's still the debate tomorrow, remember."

Chelsie nodded solemnly. "Do you still have time to go with me to see Maria Fuentes up in East Harlem?" she asked.

"Sure, I'm ready for a break from all this campaign stuff, anyway."

The two headed uptown on a fast-moving, clattering subway. When they emerged from the subway station it had begun to sprinkle.

"I hope we find this place quickly. I didn't bring an umbrella," Chelsie said.

The two friends hurried along. They passed lots and lots of little record stores playing cheerful salsa music through loudspeakers for the pleasure of passersby. The music put Nichelle in a great mood. Good music always did.

At last, they found Maria Fuentes's building, a pretty three-story brownstone nestled between a daycare center and a well-tended vest-pocket park. Maria Fuentes's apartment inside was another matter. It looked as if it had been hit by a tornado. Maria herself seemed to possess all the energy of one of those huge storms.

"My passport! Where's my passport?" she cried as she tore through a chest of drawers, tossing clothes everywhere. "I'm going backpacking in Europe, and nobody — but nobody — is gonna let me cross their borders without a passport!" Chelsie and Nichelle stood in the hallway outside the room, where she had told them to wait.

Maria upended a cardboard box on her bed. Dozens of letters, cosmetic bottles, tiny seashells, and novelty earrings tumbled out. "Aha! There you are," she cried, snatching a small blue booklet out from under a pile of fish earrings. "Henry told me that you'd be here this week," she called out to the girls. "But he didn't say what day. I'm leaving for Italy tomorrow for three months, and my sister's family is coming to stay, so I'm putting all my extra stuff in storage. I have to have the place cleaned up by nine sharp."

"What about my book," Chelsie whispered. "Have you packed it up, too?"

Nichelle could see that her friend was shaking. *Not another wild goose chase*, she thought.

"No, of course not," Maria Fuentes answered breezily. "That wouldn't make sense. Henry mentioned that you go to I. H. So I gave it to my friend's son to hold on to. He goes to I. H., too. He's a great kid. A freshman. He said he knew who you were from reading the school newspaper or something. He said he would give it to you personally."

Nichelle and Chelsie looked at each other and burst into laughter. "What's your friend's son's name?"

"Vittorio di Franco. Do you know him?"

"No, but I guess we will soon," Chelsie answered.

"I'd invite you for coffee, or tea — I noticed your accent. But I've already packed my dishes."

"We should be going, anyway. Thank you so much for your help, Maria," Chelsie said.

Back on the street, the girls did a little dance. Chelsie was grinning.

"Oh Nichelle, this is crazy. I've chased all over New York City for that book, only to find that it was heading right back to me."

"Only in New York," Nichelle said with a sigh.

Chapter 9

Friday, the 13th: The Great Debate

That night, Nichelle got a bad attack of the jitters about the next day's debate. She paced and paced, thinking of last-minute details.

Shawn seemed concerned. "Listen, sis, you need to calm down. This isn't the most important thing in the world, you know."

"You're right. But it is important to me. Andy would make a great vice president and I'd really hate to see him lose just because he isn't part of a clique. And I just want to *show* them — you know what I mean?"

"I know exactly what you mean," Shawn agreed. "You go for it."

Nichelle looked through all her campaign notes once again. She decided to call Andy for a last-minute strategy session.

Andy picked up the phone. "*S'Andy. S'uppp?*" The squawks were back. They sounded different, though. *Was that a drum in the background?*

"Andy," she said, "I just want to make sure your speech is in good shape. Are you feeling good about it?"

"*Don' worry 'bout a thing.*"

"Because, it's really important to stick to one message, you know, keep it simple, and —"

"*S'all under control,*" Andy said. "*Put y'feet up. Chill, duude. Ev'rythin's cool.*"

He sounded so confident, Nichelle immediately relaxed. After all, it was his speech, and he wasn't worried at all.

"Okay," she said. "See you tomorrow. Knock 'em dead."

After they'd said good-bye, she dialed Tori's number. "I'm just calling to ask you if you'll be on hand backstage during the debate to give Andy moral support," Nichelle said.

"Already taken care of, Nichelle. Evan and I will be there — skateboards at the ready. But don't worry, Andy will be fine."

"I just hope those debaters don't eat him alive," Nichelle answered.

At last, it was the moment she'd been waiting for and dreading. The debate. The auditorium was packed. Lots and lots of kids carried big Megan posters. *Why didn't we think of that?* Nichelle fretted.

Backstage was bedlam. About fifteen debaters were clustered around Megan, reviewing her strategy with her. Ashley Burt and Max Sklar, the quieter two candidates, paced nervously, murmuring to themselves.

Andy hadn't even shown up yet. Nichelle, Evan, and Tori were each posted by a door, waiting.

On stage, Principal Simmons announced the candidates and outlined the rules for the debate. Each candidate would have up to eight uninterrupted minutes to speak. Afterward, there would be time for rebuttals, if the other candidates wanted to respond.

Megan was first. She was dressed in the coolest outfit, a gray flowered skirt with a net skirt over that and a gray cotton sweater. Gray-and-black platforms completed the look. When she walked to the podium, kids burst into cheers. She gave a small smile and began her talk.

"Principal Simmons, fellow students, today I want to share with you some of my ideas about the importance of school government here at I. H. We all know that the job of student government is to support the administration. I believe that is an important goal.

"I would like to tell you my other goal, one that is very important to me personally. I want the student government to continue to help clubs and sports teams raise money for their activities. The clubs and activities are important to us all. How to raise money is an important question. I suggest a bake sale, and . . ."

Nichelle hadn't heard anything that boring in her life. It didn't matter. The kids loved it. They cheered every time Megan paused. *I guess it's business as usual — the cliques run the school,* Nichelle thought ruefully. She glanced at the door. Where was Andy?

Max and Ashley gave nice short speeches, but the audience was indifferent.

Campaign Chaos

To Nichelle's relief, Andy arrived near the end of Ashley's speech. He looked wonderful. The haircut, the suit, the briefcase. *Briefcase?*

When Andy stepped up to the podium, there was a gasp from the audience. His haircut had been under his hat on Thursday, so it had the maximum impact now.

Andy cleared his throat and looked straight out at the audience. Nichelle had butterflies in her stomach. *This was it.*

"Good morning, everyone," Andy began. "I am here to ask you *not* to vote for me for vice president of the student council." He paused. "Don't vote for me if you think that high school students can aspire to no higher than a bake sale. Don't vote for me if you think that only a certain group should have input into how our school is run. Don't vote for me unless you want change.

"I believe that student government here at I. H. should serve as a model for change and social good. Those who serve on the government have an obligation not to exclude, but to include. Not to take, but to give. Sports and clubs are important, certainly, but there are larger issues at stake in the lives of today's high school student. Too often I see judgments being made on the basis of very super-ficial characteristics. Too often I see us ignore the community in which we go to school.

"How many of you have noticed the homeless people who sleep in the park by the subway sta-tion? Those of us who skateboard in the park know these people. They were like us once — kids who went to school, who dreamed, who had their whole lives ahead of them. I challenge students at I. H. to take a role in changing the face of our neighbor-hood.

"How can we, mere high school students, deal with such a large problem? By working together and by remembering what is really important: what links us to others, not what drives us apart. When we do this, we will provide a model that will inspire. I have found a way to get this project started."

Andy reached into his briefcase, pulled out a CD, and held it up. It glinted rainbow colors in the spotlight.

"My CD, *Dangerous Times*, is coming out next week on the Boarders label. I created it with my best friend Evan Hadden. Our contract stipulates that ten percent of our earnings from this release will be donated to I. H. charitable projects."

The crowd started to cheer, but Andy held up his hand.

"Remember," he cautioned, "this is just the beginning. The project will grow and improve only if lots and lots of you get involved. We can't leave the running of student government to the few. I invite you *all* to participate in the life of *our* school. So remember: By casting a vote for me today, you're not just voting for Andy Groebner, you're voting for yourselves. Get involved. There's a place for everyone here at I. H., dudes. And I know that student government can lead the way."

There was no way that Andy could stop the cheers that were coming from the students now. It was amazing. Everyone was yelling and waving their arms in the air.

Well, not quite everyone. Nichelle saw Thomas, off to the side, giving Megan a very serious consolation hug.

After a few minutes, it was clear that the cheering was drowning out any possibility of a rebuttal period. Nobody was going to step forward to try arguing with Andy. Principal Simmons dismissed the assembly, reminding the students to vote. "The results of the election will be announced right here, after last period," she shouted over the din.

For the rest of the day, Nichelle was a nervous wreck. She voted at the ballot boxes outside the cafeteria and then went inside for lunch, but she just couldn't face "Friday Franks 'n Fresh Fruit." Andy *had* to win, she thought. Someone had to change this cafeteria food.

Andy seemed cool as a cucumber. Back in his regular baggy clothes, he spent his free time boarding in front of the school with Tori, Evan, and some other friends.

The second assembly was as crowded as the first. It looked like no one had left school.

Principal Simmons said a few words about the importance of the democratic process, praised the candidates for the quality of their campaigns, and then announced the winner. "Ladies and gentlemen," she said, "I give you your next student council vice president . . ." Here she paused to open an envelope and read from a piece of paper.

"Andrew J. Groebner!"

The crowd cheered. Andy stepped up to the mike to give his acceptance speech. "*Duuuudes!*" he said. "*Let's* do *it*!"

Andy went on to urge everyone to get involved. Finally, he ended with thank you's. "I want to thank Evan Hadden and Tori Burns for sticking with me. Lara Morelli-Strauss for her great graphics on my web page. I want to thank Barbie Roberts for hours of elocution lessons. Barbie, you're the best, man. But my deepest gratitude is owed to Nichelle Williams, my campaign manager. Thanks to her I was able to deliver a 'boarder's message dressed in Ivy-League clothing. Nichelle has always believed in me and my message. 'I. H. is for — '"

The entire assembly shouted the last word: "*EVERYONE!*"

Chapter 10

Party Time

At the Williamses' brownstone, everything was ready. The fridge was bursting with sodas and juice. The pizza would be delivered at eight o'clock. Everything was dusted and polished.

Barbie, carrying a big bouquet of flowers, was the first to arrive. "For the victor. Well, at least for the victor's campaign manager," she laughed.

Soon the house was filled with high school students. Everyone was in a great mood. Chelsie arrived, a little late, with a good-looking, dark-haired boy in tow, whom Nichelle recognized vaguely from the cafeteria. "This is Vittorio di Franco," said Chelsie. She gave Nichelle a tiny wink when Vittorio wasn't looking.

When Andy arrived, everyone burst into loud cheers. *"An-dy! An-dy!"* they chanted. He gave an embarrassed little bow.

Then he handed Nichelle a package. It was a copy of his CD.

Nichelle smiled. "Thanks, Andy. Should we play it now?"

"First, look at it a lil' more closely," Andy answered. He pointed at the front cover.

Nichelle couldn't believe it. Printed right on the front cover below the title it said, "For Nichelle, with thanks."

Nichelle felt tears come to her eyes. "This is so sweet. I can't believe you did this. Thank you. This campaign has been wonderful. I've learned so so much. Now let's play this!"

When the CD had been loaded and "play" had been hit, Nichelle couldn't believe her ears. What great music! A strong beat and really amazing instruments playing the tune. "This is awesome. How did you do this?" she asked.

Andy explained that he'd used various household sounds and sampled them, then played them back and redigitized them until the sound was smooth and mellow. *"My recordn' studio is in my house,"* he told her.

So that's what all that strange squawking had been in the background. The beginnings of this great music, Nichelle thought.

Lara brought Nichelle a package, too. She had framed one of the campaign posters. "I hope you like it," she said.

"Like it? It's wonderful. I'll hang it right over my desk. Thank you so much."

Later, Chelsie pulled Nichelle aside. "Look what I have — safe and sound," she said, pulling the long-lost poetry book from her bag. "I went over to Vittorio's house in Little Italy right after school. He's really nice. He gave me the book and then invited me to a great little restaurant for cannoli and coffee. Isn't he cute? He loves poetry, too. We're going to a reading tomorrow in the Village."

"Your book in the cab was almost like a note in a bottle, wasn't it?" Nichelle asked her smiling friend.

Chelsie giggled and hurried back to Vittorio.

About half an hour later, the doorbell rang. Nichelle answered it to find Thomas and Megan standing on the front stoop. She had invited them in the spirit of good sportsmanship, but hadn't really expected them to come. She was glad they had, though.

"Welcome. Please come in."

Thomas shook Nichelle's hand. "Congratulations on a well-run campaign," he said.

"That goes for me, too," added Megan.

"Thanks," Nichelle replied.

"Where's Andy?" Megan inquired. "I want to congratulate him in person."

Nichelle pointed toward the sound system, and Megan headed off in that direction. "I also want to talk to him about working on the homeless project," she called over her shoulder. "That will look great on my record for college."

Thomas lingered for a moment. He had a sheepish look on his face. "I guess it wasn't the best idea, working on my own girlfriend's campaign," he said.

Girlfriend, thought Nichelle. So, it was true then. Well, it was just like Thomas to have strung her along without saying a word.

"Working on her campaign wasn't wrong," Nichelle replied. "Not being honest with me about your intentions was."

"I-I'm sorry," Thomas said. "I behaved badly."

Nichelle shrugged. "I won't say you didn't," she began. "But look — this is a celebration party. The election's over. What do you say we put all that stuff behind us? Deal?"

"Deal," said Thomas, smiling. "You really are an amazing person, Nichelle."

After a few hours, the party wound down and everyone began heading home. It had been a long, hard week and a long, great day.

The next morning, Nichelle headed to the park to meet with Ana for their run. It was a bright, clear morning. And though it was cold, there were signs of spring. The trees and bushes had that swollen look that they get just before buds appear. And there were a lot more people out in the park than usual.

Nichelle sat on "their" bench to enjoy the sunshine while she waited for Ana. A couple of minutes later, Ana arrived with three other runners.

"Hi, I hope you don't mind, I brought along some friends. This is Mikel. He just moved here this year from Chicago, and this is his first run in Central Park. It's a great day for it, isn't it?"

"It certainly is. Nice to meet you," Nichelle said to the tall, athletic, handsome boy.

Ana continued, "You already know Sheryl and Katherine, I think, from my swim team."

"Hi." Nichelle beamed.

"Amazing campaign, Nichelle," Sheryl said. "Everyone I know can't wait to get started on the new homeless project. Andy's so cool."

"He is, isn't he?" Nichelle answered. "He's even better when you can understand him."

"Is Andy your boyfriend?" Mikel asked.

"No, he's just a good friend," Nichelle replied. "I don't have a boyfriend — right now."

At the end of the run Mikel said, "This has been great. Can I tag along next week, too?"

"Sure," Nichelle said, smiling. "That'd be nice."

Later, at home, Nichelle took the time to write to Niecy.

Dear Niecy,

This letter is coming to you from the happiest girl in New York City. I helped a friend campaign for student government and guess what? He won! Can you believe it? Not only did he win, he's going to do a really good job. Even Shawn thinks so. And you know what a tough customer he is.

I am so glad that the campaign is over. Now I have time to devote to other stuff. Like running. Today I went on my regular Saturday run and the cutest guy came along. His name is Mikel, and he just moved here. He's a great runner and he's really into nature. He could tell us the names of every bird and flower we passed. He asked why there is no ecology club at school. I think it would be way cool to start one, don't you? When you come visit this summer you'll have to go running with us. You'll love Central Park.

Love and many hugs,
Your cousin,
Nichelle

TURN THE PAGE TO CATCH
THE LATEST BUZZ FROM
THE *GENERATION BEAT* NEWSPAPER

ELECTION FEVER SWEEPS I. H.

Election fever is sweeping through International High, and the whole school is caught up in the race for student council vice president. Current vice president, Matt Choy, has announced that he and his family are moving to Brazil. Therefore, an emergency election has been called by Principal Simmons to fill this important position.

Four candidates have been nominated: Megan Graham, a junior; Max Sklar, a senior; Ashley Burt, a sophomore; and Andy Groebner, also a sophomore. But many at I. H. believe that the real race is between Megan, a member of the debate team, and Andy, known to most everyone at I. H. as a 'boarder.

Principal Simmons has scheduled a debate to take place on Friday, the 13th, with voting to follow. Results will be posted at the end of the day.

Candidates have been busy campaigning, and they're hoping all the posters, cookies, web pages, buttons, and sticky notes stamped with campaign slogans will attract voters. "It's going to be a close race," commented Principal Simmons, "but win or lose, what really matters are the issues raised by each candidate."

RUNNING FOR OFFICE

Like International High, almost every junior and/or senior high school has a student government, with students serving as elected officials. Elections take place at the beginning of the school year, giving the elected student ample time to serve in office. But from time to time, an emergency election will take place (as was the case with Matt Choy at I. H.).

A student government consists of a president, a vice president, a treasurer, and a secretary. Typically, the president oversees the student council and serves as the primary contact between students and school administrators; the vice president usually provides support to the president and initiates special projects; the treasurer oversees the student budget; and the secretary takes notes at student council meetings. Of course, these roles are flexible, and differ from school to school. At your school, it may be the secretary who has the most responsibility!

If you like working with your classmates and talking with school administrators, you should think about running for a student office. It's a great way to make friends. But most importantly, a good school officer can really make a difference in the quality of school life!

SOME POINTERS IF YOU DECIDE TO RUN FOR OFFICE:

• First, decide why you're running. Maybe your school has a strict dress code that you want changed. Or maybe freshmen and sophomores aren't allowed to attend dances, and you think that's unfair. Making a declaration of the principles and ideas you stand for when running for office is called establishing a *platform*. Your platform is really important, because it's often the main reason why people decide to vote for you.

• Ask your friends to help you with your campaign. It's a lot of work running for office, so form an election committee. You and your friends can work and have fun at the same time!

• Every school has its own procedures for elections, so talk to the student advisor or a teacher about how candidates have campaigned in the past.

• Publicize your candidacy. Make posters that announce you are running for a student office. Be sure your name appears in large, bright letters, and don't be shy about posting these notices all over the school. Flyers with your name and picture are also a great idea. Have your election committee help distribute flyers.

• Talk to your voters. A poster is a great way to let people know that you are a candidate, but there's no substitute for getting to know each of your voters personally.

• Run a fair race. Always avoid making negative comments about your opponent, even if what you're saying is true. You want people to vote *for you*, not against someone else.

Have fun! And always remember what Mr. Toussaint says:

WRITING = HONESTY = TRUTH!

Be Sure to Read All Twelve
Generation Girl Books

And Look for More Great
Generation Girl Titles to Come!

GO TO **generationgirl.com**
FOR MORE INFORMATION ON THE
GENERATION GIRLS
AND
CHECK OUT THE GENERATION GIRL™
DOLLS AT A STORE NEAR YOU!